I'M STICKING WITH YOU

For Gabriel – who is brilliant in every way,
and whom I love un**bear**ably much – S.P-H. xx

This book is dedicated to chipped teacups everywhere – S.S.

SIMON & SCHUSTER
First published in Great Britain in 2020 by Simon & Schuster UK Ltd
1st Floor, 222 Gray's Inn Road, London WC1X 8HB

Text copyright © 2020 Smriti Prasadam-Halls
Illustrations copyright © 2020 Steve Small

The right of Smriti Prasadam-Halls and Steve Small
to be identified as the author and illustrator of this work has been asserted by them
in accordance with the Copyright,
Designs and Patents Act, 1988

A CIP catalogue record for this book is available from
the British Library upon request

ISBN: 978-1-4711-8607-3 (HB)
ISBN: 978-1-4711-8281-5 (PB)
ISBN: 978-1-4711-8282-2 (eBook)

Printed in China
3 5 7 9 10 8 6 4

I'M STICKING WITH YOU

Smriti Halls and Steve Small

SIMON & SCHUSTER
London   New York   Sydney   Toronto   New Delhi

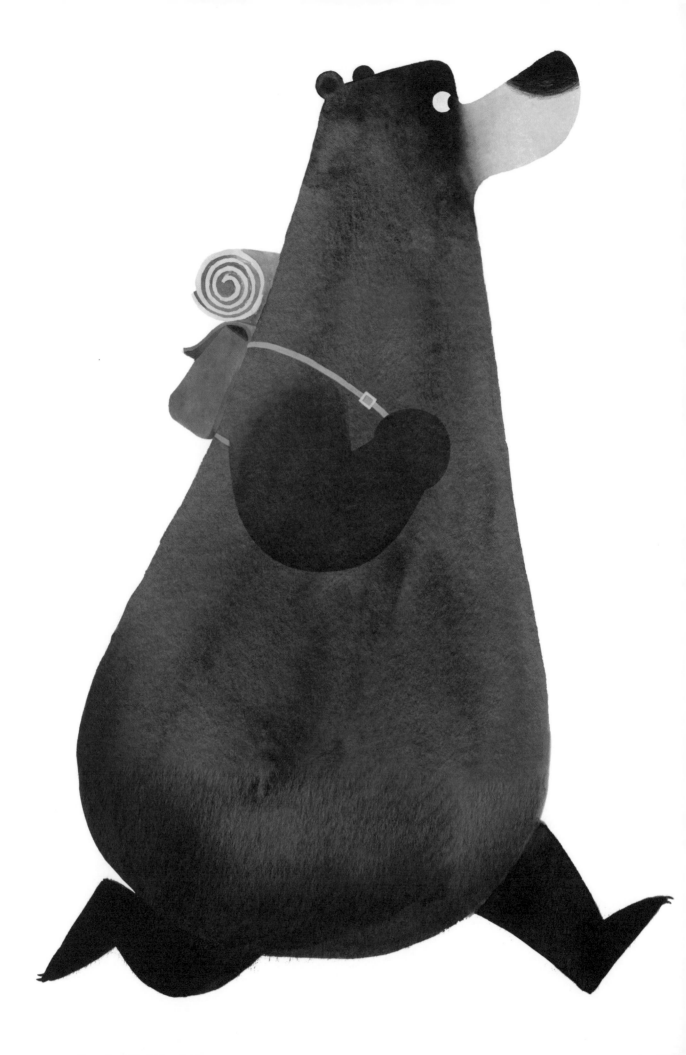

Wherever you're going,
I'm going too.

Whatever you're doing,

I'm sticking with you.

Whether you're grumpy,

or silly,

or mad,

Good times . . .

. . . and bad times,

happy or sad.

Whatever you're thinking,
I am ALL EARS,

I'm ready to listen to
ALL your ideas.

Ready to be there to help you along . . .

even if sometimes it goes a bit wrong.

Whatever you're doing . . .

THAT is the plan.

You may think I can't, but I bet you I can.

Because I will try things that I *never* would do . . .

Never, that is, until
YOU showed me to!

Like peas in a pod,
you and I fit,

Like strawberries and cream,
we are a hit.

Whatever the game,
I'm on your side.

No mountain too tall,
no river too wide.

We sit by the clifftop,
we sit by the lake,
We sit by the ice cap.

I eat all the cake.

We . . .

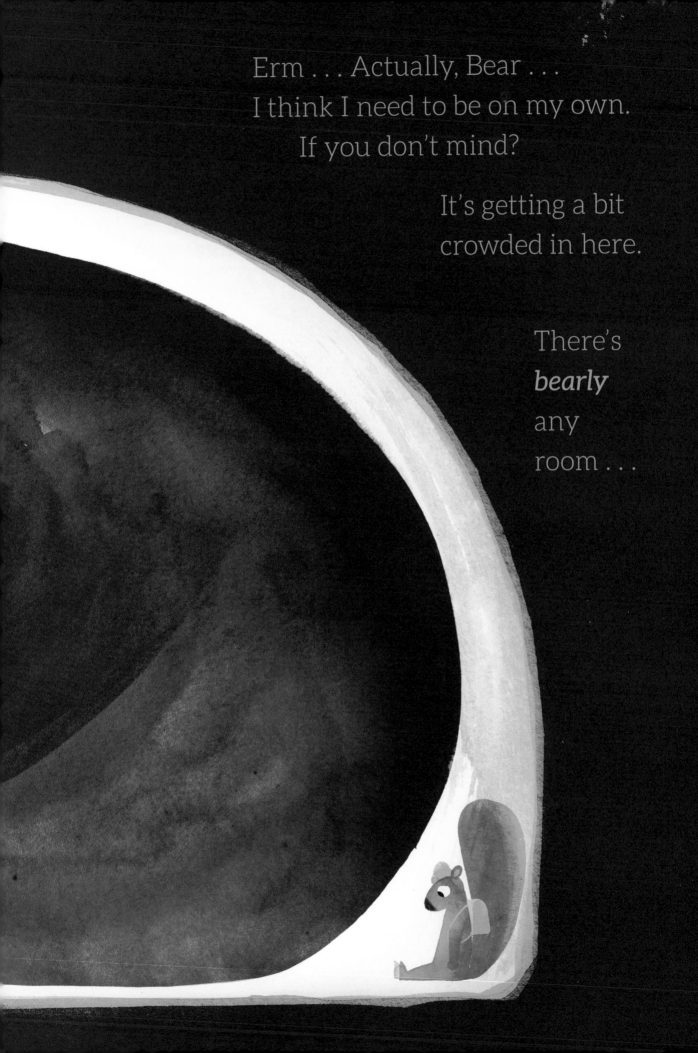

Erm . . . Actually, Bear . . .
I think I need to be on my own.
If you don't mind?

It's getting a bit
crowded in here.

There's
bearly
any
room . . .

Really . . . ?

You *sure*?

Oh.
Ok then.

Ah! That feels better,
each thing in its place,

All neat and tidy,
there's so much
more space!

I can do what I fancy,
whenever I wish,

Nothing's a squash and
nothing's a squish.

It's such a nice change to
do things alone . . .

Whatever I want to . . .
all on my own . . .

I've got all I need . . .
I don't have to share . . .

Everything's perfect . . .

. . . except . . .

. . . I MISS BEAR!

Actually . . .
Hey, Bear!
(*Bear . . . Bear . . . Bear . . .*)

Come back!
(*Back . . . back . . . back . . .*)

Who am I kidding?

Where would I even BE without you?
Who else would listen?

What would I do?

Who helps me be the best I can be?
Who shares their very last chocolate with me?

Me without you?
It just doesn't work.

Me without you?
I'd just go berserk.

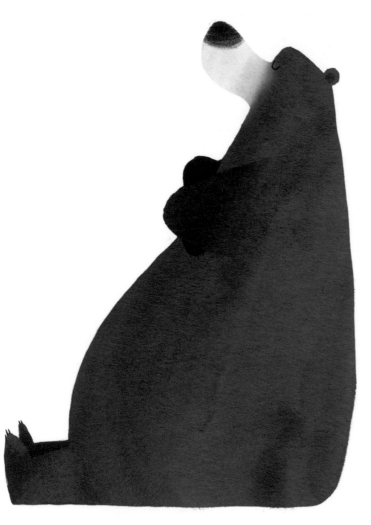

So lump it or like it,
YOU'RE stuck
with ME.

For better or worse,
it's the way
it should be.

Whether we're losing

or whether we win,

We'll be there together
through thick and through thin.

We'll pick up the pieces,

we'll patch up the hole,

We'll mend what needs fixing,

because that's how we roll.

When we're unstuck,

we won't fall apart,

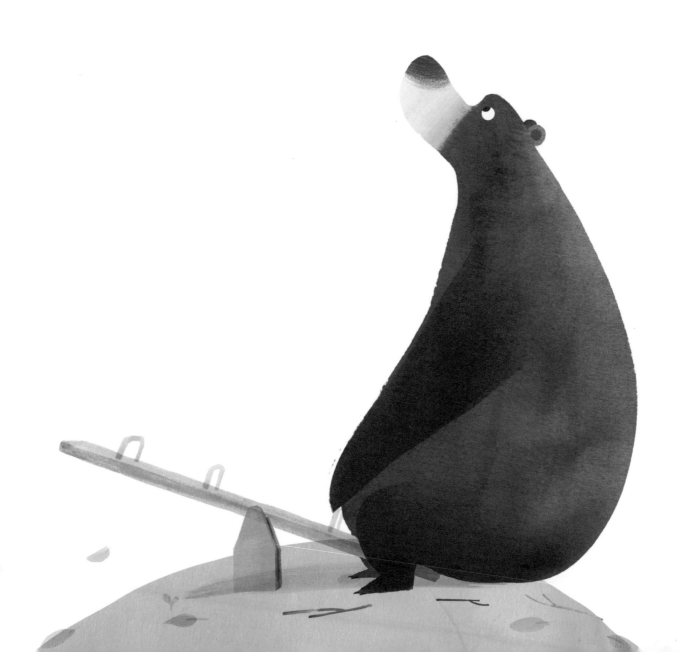

How could we ever?
We're joined at the heart.

We fit back together like
bugs in a rug,

Like jam in a doughnut,

like arms in a hug.

SO . . .
wherever you're going,
I'm coming too,

Whatever you're doing,
I'm sticking like glue.

And whether you like it,
or love it, or not . . .

We are a team . . .

. . . and
I LOVE
YOU

A LOT!